THE UNBELIEVER &
THE INTRUDER
BY MORGAN K. TANNER

A SHORT SHARP SHOCKS!
BOOK

BOOK 39

PRAISE FOR
THE UNBELIEVER & THE INTRUDER

"Felt like a nightmare, very dark and disturbing but really well written!"
– S.J. Budd (via Goodreads)

"A delightfully twisted and gruesome little addition to the Short Sharp Shocks! range."
- Zachary Ashford (via Goodreads)

"Neither of these stories is for the faint of heart, but they're certainly worth it. Morgan has a great writing style and his stories really get into your system."
- Yolanda Sfetsos (via Goodreads)

DEMAIN PUBLISHING

<u>Short Sharp Shocks!</u>

Book 0: Dirty Paws - Dean M. Drinkel
Book 1: Patient K - Barbie Wilde
Book 2: The Stranger & The Ribbon – Tim Dry
Book 3: Asylum Of Shadows – Stephanie Ellis
Book 4: Monster Beach – Ritchie Valentine Smith
Book 5: Beasties & Other Stories – Martin Richmond
Book 6: Every Moon Atrocious – Emile-Louis Tomas Jouvet
Book 7: A Monster Met – Liz Tuckwell
Book 8: The Intruders & Other Stories – Jason D. Brawn
Book 9: The Other – David Youngquist
Book 10: Symphony Of Blood – Leah Crowley
Book 11: Shattered – Anthony Watson
Book 12: The Devil's Portion – Benedict J. Jones
Book 13: Cinders Of A Blind Man Who Could See – Kev Harrison
Book 14: Dulce Et Decorum Est – Dan Howarth
Book 15: Blood, Bears & Dolls – Allison Weir
Book 16: The Forest Is Hungry – Chris Stanley
Book 17: The Town That Feared Dusk – Calvin Demmer
Book 18: Night Of The Rider – Alyson Faye
Book 19: Isidora's Pawn – Erik Hofstatter
Book 20: Plain – D.T. Griffith
Book 21: Supermassive Black Mass – Matthew Davis
Book 22: Whispers Of The Sea (& Other Stories) – L. R. Bonehill
Book 23: Magic – Eric Nash
Book 24: The Plague – R.J. Meldrum
Book 25: Candy Corn – Kevin M. Folliard

<u>Murder! Mystery! Mayhem!</u>

Maggie Of My Heart – Alyson Faye
The Funeral Birds – Paula R.C. Readman
Cursed – Paul M. Feeney

<u>Anthologies</u>

The Darkest Battlefield – Tales Of WW1/Horror

<u>Horror Novellas</u>

House Of Wrax – Raven Dane
A Quiet Apocalypse – Dave Jeffery

<u>General Fiction</u>

Joe – Terry Grimwood
Finding Jericho – Dave Jeffery

CONTENTS

THE UNBELIEVER

Was this really supposed to be fun? *Really?*

Mike's armpits were already sodden from the cramped ride in on the monorail. He'd been slapped by a fat man's tits, had his legs knocked into repeatedly by a whiney child with some kind of flashing magic wand, and was forced to inhale the aromas, coughs, and sneezes of the great unwashed that surrounded him.

The line to get in was even worse. People pushed and shoved to get in first with a wondrous sense of desperate impatience. His pass hadn't registered on the machine and it took a woman who surely couldn't be *that* smiley at this hour in the morning to rectify the card and finally allow him entry.

He'd then been accosted by a dude in a waistcoat and bowtie, holding a tablet, asking him inane questions on where he was from and what he was planning on seeing.

He only wanted to ride on a few roller coasters. And grab a massive coffee.

Mike really needed to lighten up, he knew that. But it was hard. This kingdom was far from magical in his eyes.

He stared at the domineering castle with the spiked protrusions from the busy Main Street. Admittedly the structure was impressive, as were all the buildings along the street. But then, with the amount of money they charged for admission, Mike was sure the cost involved at creating and maintaining these impressive sights hardly made a dent in the profits.

The morning sun beat down upon him with a burning intensity. The sweat poured from him, his clothes wet and uncomfortable. It only fuelled his irritability.

He spied a family of five in matching sparkly t-shirts. Their red attire enlightened everyone that this was their first trip to this magical place. He was sure glad Polly hadn't insisted on anything like that.

"Smile, Mike," she said, holding up her phone. Polly smirked at Mike's lack of excitement. "Aww, come on, you can't be grumpy here. This is the most magical place on Earth."

"Yeah, I heard."

Mike put his arm around their young niece and flashed his teeth at the camera. "How's that?"

"Well, it'll do I suppose. What are we going to do with him eh, Ruby?"

Josh and Shelley, Ruby's parents, watched the three of them. They smiled at the joy in their daughter's face whilst finding much amusement in Mike's lack of holiday spirit.

Polly and Shelley had visited this place many times growing up. It had been a family tradition and now it was time for their men to sample the magic. Ruby had been bouncing off the walls for the last three months, ticking off the days on her calendar until their 'best holiday ever' began.

Josh felt the same as Mike, but having his daughter with him had lightened his disdain for people enjoying themselves like overgrown kids.

If only it was a bit quieter, thought Mike.

"Have you seen the mouse yet, Ruby?" Mike forced a smile and ruffled her hair. She looked up and beamed at him.

"I think he's having his breakfast right now, Mike. Isn't that right, Mommy?" she said, turning to Shelley.

"I'm sure he'll be finished soon, sweetheart," she reassured her daughter. "He needs to get his strength up for all those hugs."

Well let's hope he hurries himself up so we can get back to the nice, relaxing pool.

"So how long are we going to be here for again?" Mike tried to make the question casual. "It's warm today," he added, attempting to give a reason for his question that wasn't *because I'm sick of the place already*.

He studied the crowd surrounding him. It seemed there were more excitable *adults* than children.

"Mike, don't be so silly, we'll be here all day. I can't wait to meet all the characters." Ruby grabbed Mike's hand and attempted to twirl with him. He couldn't help but smirk at her exuberance. He wasn't being *completely* serious with his derisory comments about this place. He did genuinely love seeing the look on his niece's face when she was having fun. Perhaps when he had a child of his own he would see things much differently.

He wouldn't have to wait long to find out.

It was all planned for tonight. He and Polly were to announce they were expecting a baby. Polly said this would be the perfect place to celebrate the news. Begrudgingly he could now understand what she meant. But of course, he would never admit it.

"Oh my God, oh my God, it's him. Hey, *Dogeeeee!* I *need* to get a picture with him," whined a nasally voice. Mike turned around to check he wasn't hearing things. Yes, it was a *grown woman* oozing excitement at the chance to have her picture taken with a giant cartoon dog.

"For fuck's sake," muttered Mike under his breath, "it's just a dude in a dog suit." He shook his head, eyeing the exuberant entertainer who hugged the kids and posed for pictures. There were twenty or so people lining up to 'meet' it. Mike shook his head in wonder.

Suddenly The Dog paused in its act, as if deep in thought. The plastered-on smile twitched ever so slightly. Ignoring the kids for the briefest of moments, it turned its head and stared at Mike. Its blackened eyes bore into him like twin portals to the void. It shook its head slowly. The sunlight glinted on its nose and its long ears seemed to spasm, as though they were black serpents. The Dog's teeth gleamed and Mike thought he noticed sharp points on them.

Mike suddenly felt his legs turn to jelly. He coughed, as though he'd just choked on something. He faltered backwards and only just managed to keep his footing. A panic gripped him and his breathing intensified.

What the hell was that? Did a fluffy man-dog really just throw him a threatening look?

He glanced back at The Dog, relieved to see it was now busying itself with the kids once more. The woman who'd whined to meet it was waving with an expectant grin branded onto her face. Her friends, with their fake mouse ears and sweat-drenched kids t-shirts, giggled as they took photos.

Mike collected himself with a few deep breaths. His temples were banging. This was too weird. He seriously needed a caffeine fix.

Polly gripped his hand. He looked at her, trying his best to seem calm. She smiled and nodded to a baby in a stroller, then placed her head on his shoulder. The warmth from her instantly relieved the anxiety and he relaxed against her.

"I can't wait to tell them," she whispered.

He squeezed her arm. "Me too."

"Hey, Mike, you going to get your picture taken with one of the princesses?" said Josh with a playful punch to Mike's shoulder. "Or maybe The Duck's more your thing? Polly said she'd love to see you cuddling him and kissing him on the beak, one to show the grandkids one day, eh?"

"Josh, seriously?" Mike knew his brother-in-law was joking, but Josh had always known how to wind him up. He knew Mike's thoughts on 'wondrous' places like this; they'd discussed it many times over a few beers. Josh had been looking forward to this trip for a long time, and loved jesting with Mike about how the magical kingdom of dreams would ignite his inner child.

"Your face is a picture in itself, Mike," he laughed.

"Uncle Mike's a grumpy pants," sang Ruby as she danced around him. "Don't be such a grumps, Mike. Hey, we should call you Uncle Grumple. Hey, daddy, did you hear me, I said we should—"

"*Just stop that,*" yelled Mike. It came out louder and with more fury than he'd intended. He felt awful and tried quickly to rectify the situation. "Sorry, Ruby, just trying to live up to my name, you know?" He hugged her and she squeezed him back.

"It's OK, Uncle Grumple. I forgive you, even though you are the grumpiest." She withdrew from the embrace, giggling.

Mike turned to Josh and nodded to the line of people in front of the mysterious dog.

He spoke quietly, hoping that he wouldn't draw attention from it. That face had seemed much more threatening just a few seconds earlier. Now the sneer was gone, replaced with the full-of-joy smile that Mike remembered from cartoons when he was a kid himself.

"Look at those fools, can you believe it? It's just a bloody theme park, and they're just out of work actors acting the idiots in stupid costumes for dicks like us to be wowed by. It's absolutely ridiculous. How can people be this *happy?* We're part of the problem, Josh, becoming part of this idiotic ritual designed to fleece people for as much as possible."

The whole park was cast into silence. Even the breeze had been stunned by his words. Mike thought he'd said that quietly, but obviously not quietly enough. He looked at Polly, Josh, and Shelley. Their mouths hung agape at his outburst. Ruby was welling up, fighting the urge to stop the tears.

Mike wanted the ground to open up beneath him.

"Look, guys, I'm sorry OK? It's just...I dunno, it's hot, I'm tired and really in need of a coffee. Blame it on the cocktails last night, I suppose." He braved a smile. "I really don't want to spoil this holiday, I promise. I'm...sorry."

They remained silent and avoided his eye, even Ruby. He willed them to smile again, but it seemed his words had hit hard. They'd never been offended when he'd aired these opinions back home. Maybe it was something about this place that forbade any anti-establishment comments.

Polly rubbed her belly, as though trying to shield their future child's ears from its father's lack of magical spirit.

As if on cue the music began.

It could have been from any cartoon, family-friendly movie; something where animals danced majestically in a wood, enticing the protagonist to join them in a rhapsody of colour and wonder.

The crowd sensed what was coming. Within seconds the street was cleared, with onlookers gathered on the sidewalks and in shop doorways. They clapped enthusiastically along to the music, their smiles plastered on their faces, all under some kind of happy hypnosis.

Mike spun around to look for support but suddenly he was all alone in the street.

"Polly?"

Something seemed wrong. This gleeful music should have elicited memories of happiness, but instead a cold chill shot through Mike's body. A warning sign from his mind.

Polly was nowhere to be seen. Mike's chest tightened.

A large, soft hand nestled itself on his shoulder. Heat spread across his chest and his stomach turned in knots. Mike peered up at the stranger.

A giant bear looked down upon him with large, brown eyes and a sinister smile fixated on its matted face. Mike wondered how it was supposed to be endearing to kids, for this large animal looked more like a hungry predator who'd found his puny prey. A muffled, ghastly groan emanated from within its ever-grinning head.

Was the thing salivating at the sight of Mike? He quickly rubbished the thought. He must have had more cocktails last night than he thought.

The grip tightened on his shoulder. Mike tried to pull himself away but the beast wasn't letting go. With a subtle shake of its head it guided him forward to join the carnival.

Suddenly he was surrounded by various cuddly animals—well, people in animal suits.

All had that same vacant, yet knowing grin moulded on to their costumes. Mike wondered at the torment in those faces behind the masks as they battled to look like they were enjoying themselves in this incessant heat.

The characters danced and waved to their adoring fans, who waved back with vigour. Some motioned towards Mike; his confusion bringing cheers and whistles from the excited crowd. A pretty girl in a flowing blue dress took him by the hand as the bear finally released its hold. She twirled Mike around, giggling as she passed him on to the next girl.

Surrounded by smiles and teeth, Mike felt anything but safe. He choked as his breathing rate increased in the blazing heat. He was spun around and around, passed to and fro like he was in a pinball machine. He lost his bearings with the constant motion and felt the dizziness infecting his head.

Wherever he looked was a blur of bright colours. Hands flew at him from all angles, delighting in his dumfounded fear. He tried to scan the onlookers for his family, but his eyes refused to acknowledge anything other than the dancers.

All he saw was fur, sparkling dresses, and giant, menacing hands.

Mike felt on the verge of collapsing, nausea reigning supreme in his stomach. Was this all part of the act, the classic characters revelling in the fear of a simple park visitor?

The music pummelled his eardrums. Gone were the joyous notes of celebration, replaced with a discordant whine that brought on a tinnitus-like sensation deep inside his skull.

The animals sneered and growled, Mike even felt their saliva splash across his face as the parade intensified. They snapped at his arms and he felt giant tongues licking his skin. He screamed at them to let him go, trying to pull himself away from their deplorable celebrations.

The cheering from the crowd was now deafening and Mike attempted to shield his ears from the onslaught of noise. But it was pointless. Every movement of his arms was caught by the thick, puffy hands of a man in a suit, or by the soft caresses of the princesses in their flowing dresses.

"Get your hands off me, you fuckin' maniacs," Mike screamed—his protestations were lost in the magic; a whirlwind of happiness and joy flooded his psyche like a brightly-coloured plague.

Then everything went dark.

***

Mike's head hammered him awake. He lay in bed remembering that terrible dream of his kidnapping at the hands of the happy, dancing characters. Did he really fear the place that much?

He'd had dreams that seemed real before, but this one took it to a whole new level. He could still taste the warm saliva from those savage beasts on his lips.

He reached over, his eyes still closed, and felt for Polly. But Polly wasn't there. His fingers connected with dust and small rocks.

He opened his eyes and shot to his feet, panicking.

Mike was in some kind of underground tunnel. Confusion reigned and he darted his gaze all around him to try and make sense of where he was.

A faint light from somewhere partially illuminated the place in a gloomy hue. As the realisation of his surroundings hit home he stumbled forwards, his breathing rapid, and supported himself against the rocky wall.

He didn't dare ask himself where he was, the fear of hearing his words would make everything real. The atmosphere was musty and a sharp intake of breath brought on a gravelly cough from the depths of his lungs.

Mike slumped to the ground. The stones underfoot jarred his knees and he whimpered at the unexpected jolt of sharp pain.

This must have been a nightmare, there seemed no other explanation. All Mike had to do was roll with it and soon he'd be awake in Polly's arms, stroking her pregnant belly and imagining the tiny life growing inside there.

But he knew he was kidding himself. This was real. He had to find a way out.

Mike took in a breath, lumbered to his feet, and began trudging towards the dim source of light. His eyes had now partially adjusted to the darkness. It seemed like an ancient cave buried deep underground. Was he under the park? The place was not old enough to have caverns beneath it, was it?

"Polly? Ruby? You down here?" His voice was lost in the blackened void. The sounds of the parade still rang in his ears as he ambled forwards. He shook his head to try and rid them.

Mike walked in the darkness on aching feet and tired legs. His liquid muscles threatened to give way at any moment. His breaths were amplified in this aphotic realm, the ancient walls welcoming his sounds of despair.

It was no use trying to make sense out of what was happening, how could it be rationalised? Caught in a flurry of excitement and dance, to suddenly waking up, hopelessly alone, in a cavernous prison?

This kind of shit didn't happen in theme parks.

To try and work out the details would be irrelevant, he needed to get out, and that faint light source seemed his only option.

A muffled scream radiated from somewhere. He stopped, wondering whether he was hearing things now. Listening intently he heard nothing more. Whether this was a good thing or a bad thing, he wasn't sure. But he couldn't just wait here for someone or some*thing* to find him. He had to get moving.

His need to escape was great, but Mike realised the necessity to continue with an air of stealth. If that really was a scream he didn't want to be the creator of another.

Loose pebbles crunched underfoot. Each breath seemed to escape his mouth like an exhaust pipe. He paused, composed himself as best he could, then continued.

Each step was a step closer to seeing Polly again. He yearned to rub her belly, tell her how sorry he was. And Ruby, he wanted to give that kid the best damn holiday she could imagine. What he'd give now to hear her laughing again. Mike grimaced as he tried to hold back the tears.

He'd never wanted to spoil their trip. He wasn't really the Mr Grumpy Pants Ruby had jokingly accused him of being. He was a parody of miserable if anything; willing to put up with these mild irritations in the hope of bringing joy to a young girl's heart. Plus there was the baby news. Polly could hardly contain herself; keeping it from her sister. Mike had half-expected her to have already spilled the beans, but he knew deep-down she would have needed him to be there with her.

This was *their* news.

It was in that moment he truly realised how much he loved her and how happy he was.

But the moment was over before it had begun.

A furry, slick hand grabbed his face. The stench of rot forced a violent gag. Mike thrust his arms and punched at the thing that grabbed on to him with a vice-like grip. No matter how hard he struggled, whatever had hold of him was stronger, *much* stronger.

His tongue spasmed and tried to escape down his throat as his vocal cords contracted. He coughed violently, but the sound was dampened by the giant hand that held firm.

The realisation that he was being suffocated suddenly arrived. The desperate flailing of his limbs did nothing to relieve the sensation. He was dying. His weak muscles gave up the fight, resigned to their end. As blackness invaded everything he knew, he saw Polly holding their precious baby as it smiled up at its daddy. The happiness that flowed from her was intoxicating. Had his mind been lucid, Mike would have relished his last thought on earth.

But the pain destroyed the image. The sensation of every muscle in his body cramping as one was indescribable. He was suffering the most physically and emotionally painful death imaginable. The agony seemed eternal.

***

Mike dreamed of eating. His stomach rumbled as he heard a ravenous, wet slapping sound from all around him. A deep growl joined the noise, as though a dog murmured its approval at the bone it consumed.

A dog?

His eyes flew open and he sat up with a start.

Mike sat in a large cavern illuminated with flickering torchlight. Moans, screams, and snarls echoed from the high walls; a cacophony of suffering. Joining the sound were distant roars of diabolical delight.

His head throbbed and his stomach twisted. He felt like he needed to vomit, as though he'd feasted on rotten meat. Mike's eyes stung as he stared at his new surroundings.

Everywhere he looked there were rusted metal cages. Some were empty, most were occupied. The place looked like a scene from a Third World zoo, where animals were caged and malnourished almost to the point of death. Their whole existence simply to suffer whilst pleasing their paying public.

But there were no animals in these cages.

Men sat hunched over with their heads in their hands, sobbing. Some lay supine in defeat. Others reached from between the bars in a vain attempt at escape. One man shook the metal and roared, but gave up after a few seconds and slouched back to the ground.

Mike banged weakly on the bars of his own cage and tried to scream, but his throat grated with the exertion and forcefully suggested he keep his mouth shut.

"Polly," he whimpered. Her name on his lips brought tears to his eyes. What the hell had happened to him, where was he? His thoughts were with his lady, he just hoped that whoever had brought him here had spared her. What he would give to see her now. He sat on the wet, sticky floor and forgot himself, vainly wiping away the tears with his rolled up t-shirt.

"Don't worry, man, it won't be long now," said a weary voice from somewhere.

Mike, his breathing rapid, glanced around like a panic-stricken child. "Who said that?"

"The name's Brian, though it won't be for much longer. I've seen what happens down here."

A bearded man in a ripped t-shirt and tattered shorts sat in his own cage next to Mike's, running his hand through the dusty ground. Brian's face was ingrained with dirt, the wrinkles on his forehead displayed the effects of a hard life. His eyes were sunken and his face gaunt. He didn't look over, but simply stared into the distance at nothing at all.

"Who are you?" managed Mike.

"I'm one of you, friend. An unbeliever." Brian smiled, but only with his lips. It was the sad expression of a man accepting his fate.

"What do you mean, an unbeliever?" Mike shuffled himself to the side of his cage to get a better look at the man. Rust from the cage grazed his palm, but the pain didn't register.

Brian waved a hand to the ceiling. "Up there is where people forget themselves and their problems. Magic and joy is the only thing they know in that place. But some of us cannot bring ourselves to join them in their pleasure. And that is a thing that the cast do not approve of."

"The cast? What are you talking about, *Brian*, was it?"

"It was. I've been here for a long time, it seems like years. Time forgets itself in this place." He coughed and spat on the ground. The thick globule of fluid rested on his hand, but he made no effort to wipe it off.

"I've seen them come and take us away. No one seems to resist, kinda pointless really. Where we gonna run to? Why they've left me here is a mystery, though. Perhaps I'm not ripe enough just yet."

"This is fucked, man. What the hell is this place? And what do you mean you're not *ripe* enough?"

"Friend, I really don't wish to burden you with what I know, it would do nothing to help you right now. My advice would be to sit and wait. Pray, if that's your thing, it's the only thing any of us have left."

A loud growl ricocheted along the walls from deep within the bowels of the cavernous prison. The noise rumbled through the ground and attacked Mike's thumping head.

"If only I'd known," Brian continued, "I'd have joined in more. I'd have laughed and danced and not moaned so much. The grandkids, they were having such a great time." He paused, as if reliving the memory. "There's no point in torturing myself now, though, what's done is done. This is how it ends."

Mike opened his mouth to ask what he meant, but heeded Brian's warning. Did he really want to know?

"What about Polly, Ruby? What's happening to *them*?" Brian wouldn't know who he meant, but Mike just needed to hear their names spoken again. Where were they? Were they in their own cages somewhere in this hell?

Inside himself he knew the answer. They weren't unbelievers like him. A loud roar ended his reverie abruptly, as though this place had no room for sentimentality. A man a few cages along screamed and pleaded as three men in waistcoats and bowties unlocked his cage and dragged him out.

The man kicked and lashed out with his arms, but fatigue had withered away his fighting spirit and after a swift punch to the ribs from one of his captors he simply allowed them to grab him. They pulled him to his feet and dragged him towards a dark passageway. His pathetic whimpers echoed around the cavern like desperate grief in stereo.

"Where are they taking him?" Mike whispered to Brian. But Brian didn't hear him or, more likely, chose to ignore him. The bearded man lay down and tapped his wedding ring against the bars of his cell.

Mike closed his eyes and again thought of Polly. Imagining the warmth of her smile as they told her family their exciting news broke him inside. He no longer feared what was to become of him. The fear of never seeing Polly and their baby was a sadistic torture he'd previously thought unimaginable.

A forceful metallic clunk sent a reverberation through his skull. At first he wondered whether he was dead, as surely no sound could bring with it such mental agony.

"You, on your feet," shouted a waistcoated man as he reached inside Mike's rusty cage.

Any resistance he might have had had now been lost. He felt like he'd been drugged, but it was this place, this living hell that had dissolved all of his hope. There was no defiant attempt at fighting against them, no heroic act of escape. Instead he got to his knees and crawled towards the opening of his mini-prison.

Another unbeliever accepting his fate.

"Where's Polly, is she OK?" he whispered to the ground.

"Shut it. On your feet."

Mike glanced at two empty cages opposite. The ground inside them was splattered with blood, the doors swinging on squealing hinges in a non-existent wind.

"You bastards," he muttered with no hint of aggression.

The three in waistcoats pulled Mike to his aching feet and marched him towards the gloomy passageway. His weak muscles almost failed him, but the encouraging strikes to his body served their purpose and he continued on.

A savage growl echoed around him before finally taking refuge in his head. The wet slapping noise that awoke him earlier sounded again, but this time it was amplified.

Whatever was making that noise wasn't far away now.

As Mike's legs went limp the guards dragged him like a stunned pig to the slaughterhouse. His feet trailed through splatterings of bloody viscera and bones that littered the floor. Dusty skulls watched him, the bones somehow able to translate an expression of abject fear.

"What is…where…are you taking me?"

Every muscle in his body refused to work. His veins had been infested with a fatal overdose of resignation.

"It is time to pay the price for your blasphemous ways, heathen," muttered one of the guards with a jab to his ribs.

The tunnel seemed to go on forever. Every few seconds he was struck by one of his captors. Their enjoyment of his suffering was more painful than the blows, though.

The moist growls crescendoed as Mike was thrown to the ground. He managed to turn his head, the effort stabbing him in the neck.

He lay in another vast cavern containing yet more pieces of human leftovers. Bones were piled in the corners, covered with cobwebs and giant patches of mould. Blood adorned the ground and walls, with wet speckles dancing in the dim light, as though the blood was somehow alive. The smell brought on a bout of retching and Mike's throat was suddenly scalded with the acid from his stomach.

Dead, musty, rotten flesh.

He had not even the energy to cover his nose and mouth, though he willed his body to allow him this small mercy.

A bloody corpse lay broken on the sodden ground a few paces away. The leg bones were white and ethereally illuminated as the blackened organs spilled from the torso like a ruptured beanbag. The head was missing and the pink tissue at the neck pulsated like it was still alive.

Crouched next to the body, guzzling on one of the arms, was The Duck that Josh had teased him about.

The beast's white, feathered belly was smeared red. Chunks of unidentifiable tissue clung to its body as the beak consumed the corpse's flesh. The Duck glanced at Mike, grimaced, then dropped its snack as though it had suddenly turned bad.

It sneered in a way that seemed impossible on its face and shifted towards Mike. Gone was the playful waddle that enraptured the kids above, instead it crept in an almost reptilian nature. Its eyes wide, black, and dead.

A giant snowman guzzled on a piece of pulsating red matter. Its carrot-nose dripped with thick blood as it gurgled its appreciation of the feast.

"No, what the fuck is this? Fuck, *get me out of here.*" Mike suddenly found his strength from somewhere, his body providing him with one last attempt at escape. He leapt to his feet and elbowed one of the guards in the face. But Mike had no time to savour the feeling of the nose breaking and the shriek of pain that accompanied it.

In seconds he was thrown back to the floor and kicked in the jaw. His fingers snapped as another boot crushed them. His mouth filled with blood. The anger and energy had been exterminated for good this time. His body now trembled in fear.

The Dog stood and watched the show. It held a severed head in its fluffy paw. It pulled pieces out of the face with its sharp teeth, its eyes never leaving Mike.

The men in the waistcoats stood back and laughed, watching Mike struggle on the ground. The one with the broken nose stepped forward and connected his foot with Mike's stomach. The impact brought a snigger as he held his bleeding nose.

"You're fuckin' crazy, you sick bastards, I'll kill you!" said Mike, though his threat was muffled by the blood and probably broken jaw.

"No, we are not crazy," said one of the men, crouching down to look directly into Mike's eyes. He grabbed Mike's cheeks and jerked his face to look directly at him. "The characters need to feed, how else are they to bring joy to thousands every single day? Joy and happiness are what makes our kingdom thrive. Were it not for the love from the guests we would cease to be." He shoved Mike's head away, stood, then spat on his face. "And there was you thinking they were just men in suits. You're pathetic."

Mike replayed little Ruby's excited smile in his head. How we wished he could hug her now. He willed himself to warn her, hoping his thoughts would somehow transmit through this cavern of death, up above ground to his niece's sponge-like mind.

But of course, it was a fruitless thought. His desperation had sunk to that level of hope.

"Polly," he whimpered, "I love you so much. Please take care of our baby." He felt pathetic. Quivering on the ground like a frightened child he prayed for the first time in his life. He prayed for the safety of his family. He spared not a thought for himself—in his mind he was already dead. He just hoped it would be quick.

A pain erupted in his thigh like that of a giant machete struck by the hand of a ravenous demon. Mike couldn't even manage to cry out. Perhaps the small amount of fight left in him was only there to prevent these bastards from delighting in his suffering. He'd be strong, not that it would make any difference.

The pain intensified. He howled like a dying animal.

The Duck appeared above him, red drool splashing on to Mike's terrified face. It kicked him in his ribs with a powerful webbed foot. The snarl that escaped its beak was like the roar of an indescribable hell-beast. Its eyes narrowed as it crouched, saliva and blood now flowing from its beak.

It took a bite from Mike's stomach and screamed in ecstasy as the blood erupted from the wound. The thing chewed as though it had been starving for days, pulling at his innards with hands that were surely not designed for such a horrific task.

Mike willed his mind to let go, to save him from witnessing this torment. But it cruelly denied him that small mercy.

From all around him came snarls and cheers as the cavern filled with animals and princesses, all there to share the spoils.

One of the princesses from the parade gnawed at his leg and his body spasmed uncontrollably. The snowman joined her and they embraced, sharing a bloody kiss as parts of Mike's muscle glistened on their ravenous faces.

Mike's eyes rolled back in their sockets as more flesh was torn from his body. He was paralysed, but the awful pain showed no sign of relenting. His sight was gone but he heard his skin tearing and his muscles ripping. The gushing blood sounded like he was drowning in a waterfall.

Mike wished for death, but right now it seemed a hell of a long way away. He could smell the rotten meat all around him, and the shit that escaped him as his body gave up in tiny increments.

The Dog, now finished with the corpse's head, joined its comrades in the feast. It howled like a rabid monster as it basked in the fluids of yet another victim.

As the searing pain hit its peak, like a fire blazing throughout every cell in his body, Mike finally breathed his last breath. The ritual was over. The fluffy animals and beautiful princesses calmed as they chewed on their prize.

They bowed their heads as a giant mouse entered the cavern. It strode over and examined the remains of Mike. The Mouse thrust its white hand inside Mike's rib cage and pulled out his still-beating heart. The creature held it aloft and a strange growl emanated from its smiling face. The blood spurted from the organ as it ripped it to pieces with its teeth.

The Mouse was now ready for its hug with Ruby and all the other excited little children up there, desperate to meet their hero.

The stars of the show were fed and ready to entertain once more.

But they would be hungry again.

Very soon indeed.

THE INTRUDER

The house was finally at peace. Lauren slept soundly upstairs and her gentle snores hummed from the ceiling in calming waves. She'd had a long day and Toby had insisted she go to bed early. He'd stay up to do the feeds.

He glanced up from his laptop and smiled at his newborn daughter as she slept as peacefully as her mother. Baby Josie had fallen asleep on the last bottle and, confident she was settled and dead to the world for a couple of hours at least, Toby decided he had a little time to do some of the boring accounts.

He'd been putting this job off for a couple of weeks now, convincing himself having a non-sleeping newborn would be a valid excuse.

But the taxman wouldn't be so understanding.

Every time Josie murmured or twitched he leaned forward, frightened that she'd stopped breathing or was choking, or something. Fatherhood had done little to relax him, the sleepless nights and days of cuddles to try and stave off the crying, only heightened his restlessness.

Toby felt like he could sleep for a week. His eyes were full of grit and his lids were attached to ship anchors. His face ached and his whole body cried out at him to rest.

No time to dwell on the tiredness, though. He'd been behind with these accounts and needed to get them sorted by the end of the week. Not ideal timing, but he'd make it work.

He could really do with one of his own massages.

His massage business had really taken off over the last couple of years. He'd taken a month off in order to help out with his new daddy duties, but the diary was already full for the next month after he planned to return to self-employment.

He sighed as the numbers blurred into one blackened mass of scribbles before his closing eyes. He rubbed his forehead and contemplated just having twenty minutes or so of sleep. Surely Josie would be OK without his constant watch.

He convinced himself he could do all this tomorrow, something he'd been telling himself for the last week now. A bit of rest and he'd be alert and ready to tackle the numbers tomorrow.

He closed the computer, wincing at the click it made. Everything seemed to sound louder when there was a sleeping baby in the house.

His eyes sprang open at the noise. It came from the kitchen. Toby perched himself forward on the sofa and listened. A click and a rattle. His body trembling, he held his breath.

It was someone opening the back door.

We're being fucking robbed, his instinct told him.

Toby looked at the clock; 03:11. He'd slept longer than the twenty minutes he'd promised himself. He stood on shaking legs as the clicking continued from the back of the house.

Shit. There was someone in his home. Now he thought about it, he'd forgotten to lock the back door earlier. A scratching noise crept into his ears. What the hell was he supposed to do?

Call the police? Probably the best idea, but surely the intruder would hear him and be gone in no time.

Hide in the living room and hope they left him and their possessions well alone? He'd never been a coward and never before felt this apprehension laced with anger at a stranger entering his home uninvited, planning to steal from him and his family.

He suddenly thought of Lauren sleeping upstairs and images forced themselves into his mind of the intruder doing something to her.

He clenched his fists and grimaced.

"Cheeky little bastard," he whispered to himself. Josie didn't stir, she seemed content at dreaming about—well, whatever newborn babies dreamt about.

Toby grabbed the mug of coffee that had gone cold hours ago. He downed the drink and gripped the mug, taking a deep breath.

As quietly as he could he opened the living room door and crept into the hallway.

The moon partially illuminated the kitchen and Toby's breathing almost halted when he saw what he'd feared all along. A man dressed in black was carefully going through one of the kitchen drawers. The drawer where Toby and Lauren kept their car keys, and the place they kept their emergency cash.

There was a few hundred in there. How did this robbing bastard know where to look?

Toby gripped the mug tighter, imagining it was the skull of this thief.

He paced silently behind the man in black, his stockinged feet making no sound on the tiled floor. The man was too busy rooting through the drawer to look behind him. Toby noticed the shoulder length hair as the thief methodically rearranged the contents of the drawer.

He raised the mug and without a further sound, brought the vessel down onto the back of the man's head with as much force as his tired arm could muster.

It was enough, though.

"Hey, little Josie, it's OK, sweetheart." Toby rocked his baby daughter, tapping her back to rid her body of the excess wind she'd consumed along with her bottle. She whimpered and spluttered, and after a few seconds let out a burp that Toby himself would have been proud of. "We won't let the bad man take our stuff, no no no."

Josie closed her eyes, displaying no interest in Toby's macho talk. She was fed and ready for some more sleep. Toby stood and rocked her gently, kissing her head as her snoring began. After a few minutes he braved putting her down in her recliner.

She sniffed, smiled—Toby told himself it was a smile anyway, though it looked more like a grimace—and settled down for another nice bout of sleep.

Toby watched her for a minute or so, looked at the closed laptop, and told himself he had more pressing matters to attend to.

The converted cellar was decked out with plants, scented candles, and pictures of beautiful landscapes. It had taken a while to get it like this but Toby was proud of the decor. He'd enlisted the help of Lauren, of course, the place certainly benefitted from a woman's touch.

His massage bed sat in the centre of the room in pride of place. On the wall next to it was a sink with a selection of relaxing massage oils above it. A table on the opposite wall housed a pile of soft, fresh-smelling towels. Two scented candles burned, their aroma creating a sense of calm. The place had the look of a five star hotel spar about it.

Lying on the massage table, wrists and ankles bound and mouth stuffed with one of the smaller towels, was the intruder.

Toby stepped forward and appraised his captive. There was a dribble of blood where the mug had connected, and red marks around his neck where Toby had squeezed.

The mug alone hadn't been enough to incapacitate the man, so an old-fashioned strangle hold had completed the job.

The man was still alive, and Toby metaphorically rubbed his hands with glee.

He hadn't much time; Josie might wake up at any minute and if Lauren heard her crying she may come down to see where Toby was. He had to be quick.

He slapped the man's cheeks, gently at first, then slammed his palm against his face. The man jerked his head then opened his eyes. The look in them declared panic and confusion.

"Good, you're awake," whispered Toby. The man looked up at him and it was the first time Toby saw the eyes see him. The intruder tried to cast an intimidating expression before realising he was tied up. The change in temperament brought a chuckle from Toby.

"And just who the fuck do you think you are?" said Toby, delivered with the same tone he'd ask a client where exactly it hurt.

The man glanced around the room, his eyeballs darting this way and that, silently pleading for escape.

"Look, I know you can't answer me and if I'm honest, I don't want to hear the shit that would come out of your robbing mouth anyway. I think you may have picked the wrong house, my friend."

Toby picked up a candle and breathed in its aroma. He smiled then looked at his prisoner. "I really shouldn't, it'll just send me to sleep. That's what these are supposed to do, you see? And I'm so very tired, I may even be delirious."

He tipped the wax onto the man's hand. A murmur of discomfort sounded from behind the gag and his arm pulled hard against the binding. The knot was secure enough. Smiling, Toby walked to the other side of the table and repeated the action on the man's other hand.

The eyes burned into him with hatred, as though the intruder was already planning his revenge.

Toby recognised the look. "Some people find this erotic, you know." Before his words had chance to resonate he thrust the candle into the man's cheek. His skin sizzled for a second before the flame died. A small red mark blossomed on his cheek.

"See, as I said I'm very tired right now, that's what having a newborn baby does to you. Got any kids yourself? I'm guessing not. I'm sure your thieving bastard ways are purely for your own gain, and not to share with any loved ones. Am I right?"

The man shot his head forward and growled from deep in his throat. He sounded like a wild animal attacking its prey.

"Thought so."

Toby paused and moved his ear towards the man's face, nodding in concentration as he tried to make out the words of his threat.

"There was definitely a 'fuck' in there, and maybe something about killing me?" He chuckled, "Yeah, right."

He replaced the candle on the table and headed towards the door to the stairs. "I'll be back soon."

Josie's head still had that newborn smell. Lauren had joked that she hated other people sniffing her head because they were stealing all of the smell. She wasn't really joking, though.

His beautiful daughter moved her head slightly at his touch but made no sign of waking up. Toby paused and listened. There was not a sound from downstairs. The insulation was working perfectly. It was quiet upstairs, too. Sleep would have been bliss right now, but the burglar had put paid to any relaxation plans.

As he made his way back down the stairs he heard the desperate attempts of the bound man as he tried to free himself. Toby wasn't worried, of course, a childhood in the scouts had taught him the very best knots to prevent someone from escaping.

The man halted as he spotted Toby enter the room. His eyes were wider now, as though he was now realising he wasn't going to get out of this situation as easily as he thought.

"What's your name? Huh?" Toby looked at him and placed the box of tools he'd collected from his garage on the floor. "I think I'll call you, erm," he pondered it for a moment, "Jeremy. Is that your name?" The man made no motion. "Is. That. Your. Fucking. Name?" said Toby in a forceful whisper.

The man shook his head slowly.

"Great, Jeremy it is then." He crouched down and opened the toolbox. "Listen, Jeremy, I really don't appreciate people entering my house without permission. I'm kind of old school like that, see. And what would the cops do if I called them now? You'd probably be back out on the streets in no time. And little shits like you don't like tattle-tales like me." He removed a hammer and stood, checking the satisfying weight in his hand.

"My daughter's asleep upstairs and I can't risk her life with letting you walk out of here. I love that girl with all my heart, and the thought of anything happening to her scares the shit out of me. So, with that in mind..."

The hammer smashed into Jeremy's knee cap with a sickening crunch. The intruder howled behind the gag, his whole body contorted as though he'd been electrocuted.

"See what I mean?" The other knee cap shattered with the second blow.

There were tears in Jeremy's eyes and all the gusto and attitude he'd attempted to display earlier had vanished. Before Toby lay a frightened little child. Muffled screams of agony sounded like the most beautiful concerto.

"I suppose you feel like I'm being a little harsh on you, but like I said, I'm so very tired. I'm really not thinking straight."

But he was thinking straight. When Toby had first heard the man in his house, his first thought was panic. As he smashed the mug over his head he'd felt a moral justice in his actions. It was the moment he'd placed his hands around his throat, though, that he'd been compelled to continue with this sadistic act of torture.

Was this some kind of calling? Had his whole life been leading up to this? To his exhausted mind it certainly felt like it.

As the hammer dropped to the floor, Toby felt an overwhelming sense of accomplishment. This was what he was on this earth to do.

Fathering a baby, marrying the love of his life, running a successful business; none of these came close to the righteous elevation he now felt.

"Life is good, you know, Jeremy?"

Jeremy was still conscious, but the shock of his shattered knees had seemingly sent his brain into some kind of hibernation mode.

"You still with me, you thieving fuck?" Toby slapped the intruder's face and pulled on his long hair. The head lolled to the side as he applied more force, eventually ripping a clump of dark hair from the roots. The tearing sensation in Toby's fingers sent a warm tingling to his groin. He'd never known torture could feel this good.

He ripped Jeremy's hair until his head was a bloody patchwork quilt. He stepped back and admired his work. Jeremy whimpered and stared through Toby, as though his mind had finally given up. The look both excited and saddened Toby. He was only just getting started.

Toby stood at the foot of the table and leaned forwards. Although Jeremy appeared to be letting go, his gaze still followed his tormentor.

What would he do next?

Toby grasped Jeremy's knees and squeezed. His hands manipulated the tissue that felt like a sack of marbles. Jeremy howled, the gag doing little to dampen the anguish this time.

Toby considered removing the towel and revelling in Jeremy's death throes. But he couldn't risk waking Lauren or Josie. There'd be no way to explain his way out of this. Up until tonight he'd been a regular guy. But now the torture gene had been ignited, Toby couldn't imagine an existence without this feeling.

He wiped the sweat from his brow and giggled like a schoolgirl. "This is amazing. I'm kind of sorry this had to happen to you, Jezza, but fuck me if I'm not having the time of my life. I really should be using this time to do some work, or even get some sleep. But how could I, with you down here all alone and looking so, I don't know, *ripe* for fun?"

He squeezed Jeremy's knees again. "This is better than sex."

Jeremy quivered on the table, every muscle fibre twitching as every nerve ending fired. Toby tried to imagine the agony his subject was in, but this only heightened his pleasure in being the pain-bringer.

"Wow, Jezza, I really don't know what to say." He leaned over his victim and whispered, "It's actually turning me on a little bit."

Jeremy didn't respond, his eyelids were glued shut, as if to save his mind from the visuals of this terrifying situation. Toby slapped him across the cheek but the eyes remained forcibly closed.

"Are you not listening to me?" he yelled, instantly regretting the noise. He huffed, threw back his shoulders, and marched over to the toolbox.

The Stanley knife had never been used. In truth none of the tools had been used before, Toby just wasn't a DIY kind of guy. So the blade was sharp; *perfectly* sharp.

"Keep fucking still, you piece of shit." Slicing off Jeremy's eyelids was more difficult than Toby had first anticipated. He kept thrusting his head side-to-side, preventing Toby from gaining any purchase.

Toby really didn't want to make too much mess in here, clients wouldn't react too kindly to blood stains on the walls and floor.

Leaning with his forearm across Jeremy's head he managed to hold him still enough to attack one of the lids. It didn't go according to plan, though. Blood splattered from the lacerations around his eye as his victim struggled with increasing desperation.

Eventually Toby caught a flap of skin and pulled. He roared like a primitive being as the skin tore free, then roared in anger at the state of Jeremy's face. An inch of exposed tissue now adorned the area above Jeremy's eye. The eyebrow had gone with it, too.

But at least the lid was gone and now Jeremy's eyeball had nowhere to hide. He'd stopped struggling, too.

Toby grabbed the lighter from his pocket and checked the flame. His hand shook as he watched the fire dance. The excitement was taking over.

He held the flame to Jeremy's face and tilted it towards the mushy eyeball. Jeremy struggled but Toby managed to keep his head in place; the anticipation providing him with the extra strength required. The eyeball sizzled like a juicy steak in the frying pan.

Toby inhaled the aroma with a sadistic sneer.

The guttural cry from deep within Jeremy shook the walls. His head twisted and his body pulsated up and down as though 1000 watts of electricity was being force fed into every cell. There seemed no hint of him letting up.

Toby watched with a smile on his lips, lips he was licking in delight. He really wanted to do the other eye, too but in Jeremy's present state he figured that would be a challenge too far.

The sounds were like a giant animal dying. Jeremy was being too loud. Toby clenched his fist in anger and thrust it into Jeremy's ribs. He felt a crack, but the victim didn't show a reaction. The pain hardly compared.

Annoyed with this, Toby took the Stanley knife once more and sliced through Jeremy's t-shirt. He ripped the thing in two and frowned as he stared at the objects beneath the garment.

"You fucking what? You're a woman?"

How did he not notice this earlier? Well, tiredness can do strange things to you.

Jeremy's moans became quieter, perhaps *her* mind was working well to block out the horrifying sensation.

As if just waiting for this moment, Josie's cries emanated from above.

Toby threw the blade to the floor and ran to the stairs. "You inconsiderate fucker, you woke my baby with your screaming. I'll be back in a minute." He glanced at his intruder's naked torso, "*Bitch*."

"Hey, little Josie, what's the matter?" His daughter's face was red and swollen from all the crying. He picked her up and jiggled her on the spot, listening for any sounds from Lauren upstairs.

All seemed quiet, which was strange. But this whole night had been strange.

Toby lay Josie on the changing mat and unbuttoned her sleep suit. "Let's change this bum shall we?"

The crying began again, with real tears this time. Toby had become an expert at changing nappies, especially when he felt this tired. When he'd finished he pulled a silly face with cross-eyes and tongue out, then smiled at his beautiful daughter.

"Daddy," said Josie.

Toby frowned, his heart racing in his chest. What the hell?

"Daddy."

He stumbled backwards with a thump. Toby rubbed his palms in his eyes and shook his head, trying to rid the insanity that had suddenly nestled deep inside there.

"Yes?" he whispered, his voice quivering.

"What have you done to Mommy?"

Toby picked up his daughter and snuggled his face into her neck. He closed his eyes and stumbled as sleep tried to begin its subjugation.

Josie pushed herself away from his embrace and looked at him with a tilt of her head.

"What have you done to Mommy?"

Her words echoed through Toby's skull and he shook his head to try and rid them. But she kept on with the same question over and over.

Toby placed her carefully back into her recliner and shuffled towards the door. He shook his head, with a look of disgust at what she was suggesting. His body was sticky with sweat and he panted as he tried to escape her accusatory words.

"What have you done to Mommy?"

Josie's face begged him for an answer and as Toby retreated from the room she began to cry again.

"Shut up, shut up! I haven't done…Mommy's sleeping, that's all. Lauren. *Lauren!*" He screamed for his wife, panic setting in as there was no response from upstairs.

What had he done? No, it wasn't true. He was just tired, or dreaming. Yes, that was it. This couldn't be real. The question from Josie—no, she was just a baby, and babies can't talk. Was he losing his mind? He must have been. Was any of this real?

He hurried down the stairs, neck tense and legs liquefying. What was happening to him?

By the time he reached the cellar his chest had expanded tenfold.

As he looked at the body on the table, reality took a headshot.

Toby collapsed to his knees and screamed.

"*Lauren!*"

She remained motionless.

He stared up at the ceiling and his throat burned at the exhaustion from his howls.

"No, no, no, no, what have I done?"

His eyes were invaded by tears, the salty sludge pouring over his face like a spreading infection; the symptoms of his horrific actions made flesh.

Toby crawled towards his wife. His fingers brushed against the sticky patch of carpet where her blood had collected. He held his soiled hand to his face and tasted the blood, as if trying to make sure it was all true.

The flavour on his tongue excited him and he'd never felt so disgusted with himself.

He braved standing and looked down on the tortured Lauren.

Her chest still moved faintly.

Toby stroked a stray hair from her face that had become stuck to the wound above her eye. He collapsed to the floor and doubled up with the exploding pain in his gut.

Lauren groaned from the massage table above him. Toby struggled but made it to his feet. The tears had dried. The pain had gone.

He sniffed. "I can't let you suffer any more, my darling."

His fingers fitted her throat as though they had been made for each other. As the colour drained from Lauren's face Toby smiled.

This feeling was stronger than any love he ever had for her. He wondered whether

Lauren would be pleased she was satisfying an urge he never thought existed before tonight.

He hoped she would be.

Toby closed and locked the door to the cellar just as Josie began to chuckle. He trudged into the living room and her face delighted in his presence. He picked her up and held her tight, convinced she hugged him back.

"I love you so much, my little angel." He sat on the sofa and relaxed into the cushions. "I will never let anyone come between us ever again. This is the beginning of the rest of our lives. Together we shall embrace our new calling."

Josie still smiled, although her eyes were shutting.

"Shhh, it's OK, Josie, you go to sleep and leave it all to me." He stood and placed her back in her recliner.

He settled back down on the sofa and finally closed his eyes. He relived the pain he had inflicted upon the intruder, and the warmth that flowed through his body as he realised it had been his wife all along. The sensation was pure ecstasy. He now had a taste for suffering and needed to feel that exhilaration again. And again. With Josie at his side he would continue his quest. She would understand, in time.

It was indeed the beginning of the rest of their lives.

BIOGRAPHY

Morgan K. Tanner is a writer, drummer, and golfist currently residing in the English countryside. The idyllic surroundings make it an ideal place to write, drum, and hide the bodies. The busy sound of the typewriter is perfect to drown out the hum of the antiquated torture equipment.

When not writing or inflicting pain and suffering on his numerous victims, he indulges himself in all things horror and metal.

He is the author of *An Army of Skin*, and *The Mind's Plague* and *Other Bites of Brutality*.

You can praise or indeed abuse him by visiting www.morganktanner.com or find him on Twitter @morgantanner666.

ADRIAN BALDWIN (COVER ARTIST)

Adrian is a Mancunian now living and working in Wales. Back in the 1990s, he wrote for various TV shows/personalities: Smith & Jones, Clive Anderson, Brian Conley, Paul McKenna, Hale & Pace, Rory Bremner (and a few others). Wooo, get him! Since then, he has written three screenplays—one of which received generous financial backing from the Film Agency for Wales. Then along came the global recession which kicked the UK Film industry in the nuts. What a bummer! Not to be outdone, he turned to novel writing—which had always been his real dream—and, in particular, a genre he feels is often overlooked; a genre he has always been a fan of: Dark Comedy (sometimes referred to as Horror's weird cousin). *Barnacle Brat* (a dark comedy for grown-ups), his first novel won Indie Novel of the Year 2016 award; his second novel *Stanley Mccloud Must Die!* (more dark comedy for grown-ups) published in 2016 and his third: *The Snowman And The Scarecrow* (another dark comedy for grown-ups) published in 2018. Adrian Baldwin has also written and published a number of dark comedy short stories. He designs book covers too—not just for his own books but for a growing number of publishers. For more information on the award-winning author, check out: https://adrianbaldwin.info/

DEMAIN PUBLISHING

To keep up to-date on all news DEMAIN (including future submission calls and releases) you can follow us in a number of ways:

BLOG:
www.demainpublishingblog.weebly.com

TWITTER:
@DemainPubUk

FACEBOOK PAGE:
Demain Publishing

INSTAGRAM:
demainpublishing

www.ingramcontent.com/pod-product-compliance
Lightning Source LLC
Chambersburg PA
CBHW031332130726
47988CB00007B/3100